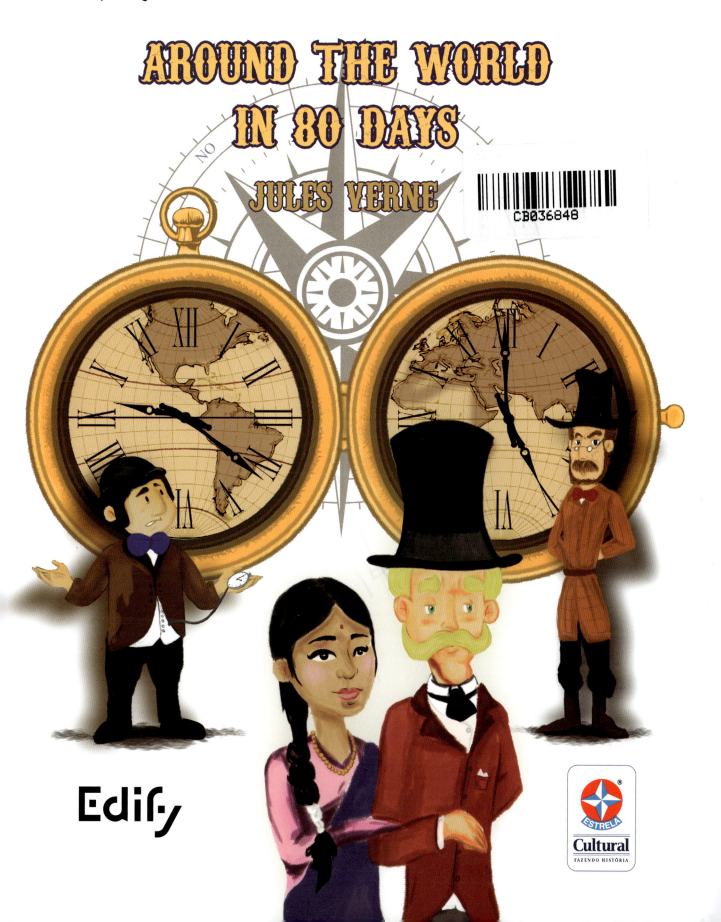

© 2019 – All rights reserved

GRUPO ESTRELA

PRESIDENT Carlos Tilkian
MARKETING DIRECTOR Aires Fernandes
OPERATIONS DIRECTOR José Gomes

EDITORA ESTRELA CULTURAL

PUBLISHER Beto Junqueyra
EDITOR Célia Hirsch
EDITORIAL COORDINATOR Ana Luíza Bassanetto
ILLUSTRATIONS Danilo Tanaka
ART PROJECT Ana Luíza Bassanetto
COPYEDITORS Mariane Genaro, Luiz Gustavo Micheletti Bazana
PROOFREADERS Felipe Guimarães, Michele Myers
TRANSLATION Michele Myers

Dados Internacionais de Catalogação na Publicação (CIP)
(Câmara Brasileira do Livro, SP, Brasil)

Junqueyra, Beto
  Around the world in 80 days / Jules Verne ; tradução e adaptação Beto Junqueyra ; ilustrações Danilo Tanaka ; versão em inglês Michele Myers. --
  1. ed. -- Itapira, SP : Estrela Cultural, 2021.

  Título original: Le tour du monde en 80 jours
  ISBN 978-65-86059-01-4

  1. Literatura infantojuvenil em inglês 2. Verne, Jules, 1828-1905 I. Tanaka, Danilo. II. Título.

21-77322   CDD-028.5

ÍNDICES PARA CATÁLOGO SISTEMÁTICO:

1. Literatura infantojuvenil em inglês 028.5
2. Literatura juvenil em inglês 028.5

Cibele Maria Dias - Bibliotecária - CRB-8/9427

Total or partial reproduction, by any means whatsoever,
is prohibited without the express permission of the publisher.

1st edition – Itapira, SP – 2021 – PRINTED IN BRAZIL
All rights of the edition reserved to EDITORA ESTRELA CULTURAL LTDA.

Rua Municipal CTP 050 Km 01, Bloco F, Bairro Quatis
CEP 37190000 – Três Pontas/MG CNPJ: 29.341.467/0002-68
estrelacultural.com.br estrelacultural@estrela.com.br

Introduction

Around the World in 80 Days is an adventure novel written by a French author, Jules Verne, in 1873. Th e work portrays the technological advances of those times. Until the second half of the nineteenth century, crossing the world was a very diffi cult thing when compared to the present day. Realizing it would be at least a feat that would lead to an unpredictable deadline, perhaps many months. However, with the emergence of powerful steamboats and the creation and expansion of railroad lines crossing territories such as India and the United States, this has become possible. Still, someone saying that could do this feat in eighty days, overcoming all sorts of challenge, seemed like a crazy idea. An eccentric Englishman named Phileas Fogg (read "Fileas", a Greek name) is challenged by his colleagues from a London club and embarks on an adventure laden with suspense. He is accompanied by the clumsy Passepartout (read Passpartu, a French name), which makes the storyline even more fun. In the adaptation of the writer Beto Junqueyra, with illustrations by Danilo Tanaka, the young reader will feel on each page this fi ght against time and space, passing through diff erent cultures at various points of the world.

Phileas Fogg, a man of few words and many mysteries

ON OCTOBER 2, 1872, Phileas Fogg lived at N°. 7 Saville Row, London. He was a man of few words and his life was a perfect routine. His every move was made according to the hands of a clock. Everything had to be done with precision. Not one second more or one second less. Such rigorousness cost his servant dearly after preparing his master's shaving lotion one day. He had heated the water to 29 degrees instead of 30 degrees. He was dismissed because of that, and substituted on the same day by a young Frenchman called Jean Passepartout.

In the midst of such precision, Phileas Fogg's life was, however, a mystery to all. Was he rich? Undoubtedly. Yet, how had he made his fortune? No one knew. Had he travelled a lot? It was likely, for he knew maps better than anyone. But where did he travel to? It was impossible to say. Did he have friends and family? No one had ever heard of them. He was a member of the Reform Club. That was all.

As usual, Phileas Fogg left his house when Big Ben struck 11.30. After walking down the same path, putting his right foot before his left foot five hundred and seventy-five times, and his left foot before his right foot five hundred and seventy-six times, the mysterious gentleman arrived at the Reform Club.

His daily routine followed the same ritual: he sat at the same table, ordered the same dish, and finished his meal at exactly 12.47 pm. Then, he went to the large hall and read two newspapers until it was dinner time. Finally, still in the same hall, at 5.40 pm, he started to read the third newspaper of the day.

Phileas Fogg seemed to be chained to his pocket watch. Or perhaps time never let him go. Nevertheless, an unexpected event could put his orderly life at risk…

A conversation that will likely cost Phileas Fogg dearly

AFTER READING THE NEWSPAPER, Phileas Fogg met with his five usual partners of card games. They were rich and highly respectable men, and they discussed the top national news headline: the incredible robbery of fifty-five thousand pounds from the Bank of England.

"I don't think they will catch the robber," said Andrew Stuart, an engineer.

"He won't get away!" broke in Gauthier Ralph, one of the bank directors. "Several police inspectors are already on his trail."

"But the world is too big!" insisted Stuart.

"Not anymore," said Phileas Fogg, in a low tone.

"What do you mean? Has the Earth become smaller?" asked Stuart.

"Absolutely! Now it is possible to go around the world in only eighty days," replied Ralph.

"It's true, gentlemen," interrupted John Sullivan, a banker. "Eighty days, now that the railroad section between Rothal and Allahabad in India has opened. Here is the estimate made by the *Morning Chronicle*:

Estimate to go around the world in 80 days

FROM LONDON TO SUEZ VIA MONT CENIS AND BRINDISI BY Rail and Steamboats	7 DAYS
FROM SUEZ TO BOMBAY by Steamer	13 DAYS
FROM BOMBAY TO CALCUTTA by Rail	3 DAYS
FROM CALCUTTA TO HONG KONG, by Steamer	13 DAYS
FROM HONG KONG TO YOKOHAMA, by Steamer	6 DAYS
FROM YOKOHAMA TO SAN FRANCISCO, by Steamer	22 DAYS
FROM SAN FRANCISCO TO NEW YORK, by Rail	7 DAYS
FROM NEW YORK TO LONDON, by Steamer and Rail	9 DAYS
TOTAL	80 DAYS

"But we mustn't forget to take into consideration bad weather, contrary winds, shipwrecks and railway accidents," exclaimed Stuart.

"No! This is all included," insisted Phileas Fogg.

"Theoretically you are correct, Mister Fogg, but in practice…"

"In practice too, Mister Stuart."

"I'll wager four thousand pounds this is impossible!" said Stuart.

"And I wager twenty thousand pounds with you gentlemen that I can go around the world in eighty days," returned Phileas Fogg.

"That is crazy!" exclaimed Sullivan.

"No, it isn't. Do you accept the wager?"

"Yes, we accept!" replied all the men at once.

"I will catch the train for Dover today, Wednesday, at 8.45 pm. I should be back in this very room on Saturday, December 21, at 8.45 pm. Exactly eighty days later. Not one second more or one second less."

Before leaving the Reform Club, Phileas Fogg even played another round of cards. It was 7.25 pm. As usual, he arrived at his house at 7.50 pm. As soon as he closed the door, he called Passepartout and said, "Pack a bag with some clothes for each of us; we leave in ten minutes to go around the world."

Passepartout, who barely had time to take in the news, set about doing what his master had asked and immediately packed the bags. They left the house at 8 o'clock and hailed a cab. The young Frenchman carried only one travel bag and one handbag full of money to cover Mister Fogg's expenses around the world.

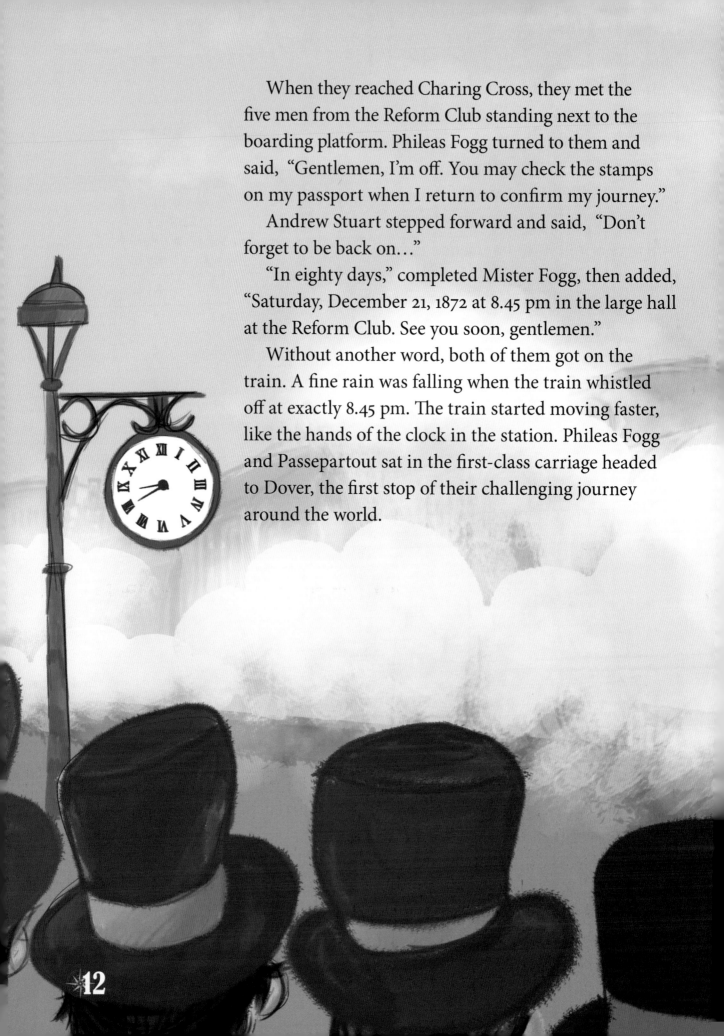

When they reached Charing Cross, they met the five men from the Reform Club standing next to the boarding platform. Phileas Fogg turned to them and said, "Gentlemen, I'm off. You may check the stamps on my passport when I return to confirm my journey."

Andrew Stuart stepped forward and said, "Don't forget to be back on…"

"In eighty days," completed Mister Fogg, then added, "Saturday, December 21, 1872 at 8.45 pm in the large hall at the Reform Club. See you soon, gentlemen."

Without another word, both of them got on the train. A fine rain was falling when the train whistled off at exactly 8.45 pm. The train started moving faster, like the hands of the clock in the station. Phileas Fogg and Passepartout sat in the first-class carriage headed to Dover, the first stop of their challenging journey around the world.

A police inspector in pursuit of an elegant gentleman

THE DAYS WENT BY. On October 9, police inspector Fix anxiously awaited the passengers on the steamer *Mongolia*, arriving from the Italian port of Brindisi. He was one of the many detectives sent to different places around the world to catch the robber of the Bank of England. Two days ago, Fix received a description of the thief: a tall elegant gentleman always carrying a top hat. He had blond hair and a long moustache that was divided exactly in the middle.

His heavy breathing was finally stifled by the arrival of the *Mongolia*. There was one impatient passenger amidst the rest who asked the inspector where the office of the English Consulate was. The passenger was Passepartout, who had to have his master's passport stamped. When Fix saw the master's picture, he told Passepartout his master must present himself to the authorities. After all, Mister Fogg looked just like the suspect of the grand theft. However, Inspector Fix needed a warrant from London to arrest him.

Passepartout returned to the steamer, and a few minutes later Phileas Fogg was in the consul's office. Fix was waiting next to the consul, who stamped his passport and released him: there was no reason to keep him from continuing his journey, as his papers were in order. The inspector was furious, but there was nothing he could do. A prison warrant would not arrive in time, so Fix could not detain him, nor did he reveal to the English passenger that he was at risk of going to jail.

Alongside Passepartout, Phileas Fogg calmly returned to the boat and boarded. Fix did not want to lose his suspect from sight, so he decided to board the *Mongolia* and sail to Bombay, one of the biggest cities in India and under British rule. Once they arrived there, he expected to receive the warrant to arrest that mysterious man, who the inspector believed was running from the police.

The *Mongolia* sailed through the waters of the Red Sea at full steam. Until then, things were going according to plan for Phileas Fogg. Time was not gained or lost during their journey from London to the Egyptian city of Suez. Everything went according to schedule: the stretch by train from London to Dover; crossing the English Channel to the port of Calais then to Paris; from the French capital, always by train, through Turin in the north of Italy to the port of Brindisi at the tip of the heel that forms the boot shape of that country; now on board of the *Mongolia* sailing through Europe all the way to Egypt. Everything going as planned. On the way to India, the ship stopped in Aden, a city south of the Arabian Peninsula, to replenish coal for the ship.

Passepartout found Inspector Fix on board the ship, unaware that he was in pursuit of his master. The inspector wanted to find more information about the Englishman's intentions. Fix became even more suspicious when Passepartout told him Mister Fogg had announced they were going on a sudden journey around the world because of a wager. His suspicions increased when the Frenchman told him about the bag full of brandnew banknotes from the Bank of England to pay for the long journey. It seemed like a crazy idea, but Passepartout followed his master's orders. He knew nothing else about the matter, nor did he want to know. To someone like him, who knew nothing outside of Europe, everything was a great adventure.

4 Propitious winds for Mister Fogg

THE OCEAN HELPED PHILEAS FOGG: the *Mongolia* moved rapidly along the currents of the Indian Ocean and arrived in Bombay on October 20, two days ahead of schedule.

Phileas Fogg had no desire to visit the landmarks of the city, nor the forts or magnificent library or lively markets, bazaars, mosques, synagogues and Armenian churches. When he set foot on Hindu soil, he simply walked to the British consulate: one more stamp to confirm his journey around the world. Meanwhile, Inspector Fix was disappointed to learn that the warrant had not arrived. He had no option but to continue to follow the untroubled English gentleman.

Passepartout, on the other hand, was excited to venture along the streets of Bombay. His curiosity took him to the splendid pagoda on Malabar Hill, which he ignorantly entered. The young Frenchman did not know that it was forbidden for foreigners to enter these temples. His presence in this sacred place enraged some of the faithful. The athletic Frenchman had to show his strength and agility as he ran out, followed by some exalted worshippers. During his escape he lost his shoes, which would later cost him dearly…

A few minutes later, the train whistle shrieked as it disappeared into the darkness of the night on its way to Calcutta, located on the opposite side of India. On board the train, Passepartout found Phileas Fogg already settled in, and occupying the seat next to him was an increasingly annoying passenger: Inspector Fix.

5 Unexpected events in the forests of India

IT WAS AN UNEVENTFUL TRAIN RIDE through the Ghats mountains and the relatively flat lands of the Khandeish country, with one stop in Burhampur for passengers to have lunch. The train travelled quickly along its course, its smoke puffing spiralling designs along the landscape. Palm trees appeared to welcome the travellers, swaying between picturesque bungalows and magnificent temples. However, when they arrived at the Rothal station, after one more day of travel, they were surprised when the conductor shouted, "All passengers must get off here!"

The passengers did not have time to complain. The conductor explained that the railroad to Allahabad was not finished. The European newspapers had been mistaken! Those who wanted to go to Calcutta and continue their journey to eastern India had to go through the forest using another means of transport.

The calm English gentleman was not troubled, for he knew the two days they had gained previously would make up for any delays ahead. They would find a way to reach Allahabad soon enough. When Passepartout went out to buy some shoes, as he was still barefoot, he found much more than a beautiful pair of leather loafers. The servant discovered an unexpected means of transport: nothing less than a ride "on board" an elephant!

Mister Fogg hired a Hindu guide who knew all the shortcuts in the area, and within a few minutes they were deep in the Indian forest. Phileas Fogg settled in the back of the howdah and their luggage was placed in the front.

The elephant marched on uneventfully while Passepartout bounced up and down as if he were in a circus. Monkeys watched them and made funny faces, as if making fun of the Frenchman and his crazy 'acrobatics'.

They travelled a long distance through the dense forest; it looked like a green tunnel from which it was difficult to distinguish night from day. Suddenly, they heard a sound that was not part of the forest symphony. The sound that echoed through the trees seemed to march in their direction, then it turned into a scary rhythm which startled the elephant to a stop. After a few minutes, they watched a procession of fanatics, screaming and beating their drums. Men armed with spears were carrying a lovely young lady covered in jewels and wearing a gold studded tunic. She appeared to be unconscious. The guide knew about the barbarities committed by this cult, so he hid the elephant behind some plants and whispered to the passengers, "This is a ritualistic sacrifice. The story of this woman is wellknown here. She is called Misses Aouda, and she must be burnt alive next to her husband's corpse, the rajah, who died a few days ago. The sacrifice will be held tomorrow at the break of day."

"We must save her," said Phileas Fogg, looking at his pocket watch, without losing his calm. "I'm twelve hours ahead."

A remarkable and dangerous rescue

HOURS LATER, MISTER FOGG, Passepartout and the guide tried to enter the temple to rescue the young Hindu woman, but there were many guards watching the rajah's widow. There was nothing they could do. Mister Fogg considered using the elephant to release her from her captivity, but how? As he walked with the guide back to the animal, Passepartout disappeared.

The gongs sounded the beginning of the ceremony. The young Hindu woman was carried to a pyre to be burnt next to her husband's corpse. A guardian lit a torch to set the wood on fire. Suddenly, to everyone's horror, the corpse rose, lifted the young woman in his arms and ran towards the elephant. The fanatics were terrified of what they believed to be a powerful deity, and they prostrated themselves on the ground and dared not lift their heads. The 'deity' who was wearing the resuscitated rajah's clothes, approached the animal and announced, "Let's get out of here!"

The odd figure stood before Mister Fogg and the guide, and revealed his true identity: it was Passepartout dressed as the rajah.

He leapt onto the back of the howdah with the still unconscious young woman.

"How did you do that?" asked the terrified Hindu guide.

"I had to hide the corpse, put on the rajah's clothes, and play dead next to…"

Before he could finish his sentence, his trick was discovered by the fanatics, who were running towards the elephant amidst terrifying screams. Dodging bullets and arrows, the group riding on the brave elephant disappeared into the forest.

They arrived in Allahabad after a bumpy, yet without any more scares, ride, then took the train to Calcutta. Misses Aouda was slowly recovering her senses. Phileas Fogg convinced her to go to Hong Kong with them to protect her from any retribution from the religious fanatics. She told them she had relatives who lived in that city nestled on the Chinese coast, a city that also belonged to the English crown.

7 A trial in Calcutta

AFTER PASSING THROUGH THE RELIGIOUS CITY OF BENARES and entering the sacred valley of the Ganges River, the train arrived in Calcutta. It was exactly 7 am on October 25, twentythree days after they had left London. Phileas Fogg was within the schedule he had planned. He had not gained or lost any time. However, as they stepped off the train, an awful surprise happened: a policeman arrested Passepartout and Mister Fogg! The servant was accused of having entered a Hindu temple in Bombay, which was forbidden, so he had to go to trial. His master also had to go! After all, Phileas Fogg was responsible for his French servant's inadequate behaviour.

The reason they were taken to the authorities was Inspector Fix: he had plotted everything. He thought he could arrest the thief now that they were in Calcutta, an English settlement, and he hoped he would get a warrant in a couple of days. He had to delay Mister Fogg. While the gentleman was engaged in saving the young widow, Fix had enough time to convince the religious Hindus to accuse the gentleman and possibly arrest him in Calcutta. And as proof, they produced the shoes Passepartout had left behind while escaping from the temple!

Would they be able to defend themselves from the accusations? Would there be enough time to reach the ship that was ready to set off to Hong Kong? Or would this be the end of Phileas Fogg's journey?

They were judged and condemned in the Hindu court according to their local laws, and Mister Fogg had to pay a large sum of money for their bail and release.

This was the only way they were able to arrive at the harbour on time and depart on the steamer *Rangoon*. Since Fix had still not gotten a warrant for the arrest, his only choice was to discreetly follow the gentleman. But…

The English ship was built of iron and had a huge propeller. It cast off to Hong Kong one hour later, at 12.00 pm, October 25. Phileas Fogg was neither behind nor ahead of schedule. He was still in command of the hours, minutes and seconds. And, next to him, there was a lovely young Hindu lady whose heart was beating as strongly as the hands of his watch.

Uncertainties at sea and on land threaten Phileas Fogg's plans

THE *RANGOON* STEAMED THROUGH THE WATERS OF THE INDIAN OCEAN, stopping quickly in Singapore to replenish its coal supply. On board of the ship, Fix remained hidden from Mister Fogg and Passepartout. He could only peer through the window of his cabin, and his mind was assaulted by many questions: why was this lady travelling with his suspect? Had the English gentleman travelled to India to pick her up? Where they conspiring together? Fix could not wait to arrive in Hong Kong, which was governed by Britain and where he would finally get his warrant and arrest the eccentric Englishman.

Mister Fogg had no idea that a policeman was tracking him as the robber of the Bank of England. Meanwhile, Misses Aouda was becoming more acquainted with the man who led the rescue mission that saved her life.

But as they navigated the high seas, Passepartout inevitably stumbled upon Inspector Fix, who decided to warn him about his master's true intentions on this journey. The Frenchman could not believe such accusations, and he concluded that the inspector was working for the members of the Reform Club, who sent him to follow his master to make sure he did as agreed upon for the wager!

The *Rangoon* arrived in Singapore half a day ahead of schedule, according to calculations made by Phileas

Fogg. It was October 31. Time was in his favour, so he decided to take Misses Aouda for a carriage ride around the island. The landscape was lined with palm trees and adorned with blooming clover trees that appeared to reflect the beauty of the lovely lady.

At 11 o'clock the *Rangoon* cast off loaded with coal and headed to Hong Kong. The ship travelled so fast that a few hours later its passengers could no longer see the mountains of Malacca, where the world's most beautiful tigers roamed.

The sea began to change its behaviour. Sometimes it rolled out angry storms, and other times it was so calm that not even a trickle of wind blew to help the *Rangoon* sail. As a result, they arrived in Hong Kong on November 6, one day behind schedule!

Luckily, the ship taking them to their next destination was late. In fact, the steamer *Carnatic* was being repaired and it would only leave the following morning.

The extra time was exactly what Mister Fogg needed to deliver Misses Aouda safely to her relatives. He went to the Trading Centre and discovered that her cousin, whom she expected to meet, had moved to Holland some time ago. There was nothing left to do but invite the Hindu woman to go with him to Europe.

"I do not want to intrude, Mister Fogg!" said the young lady, somewhat embarrassed.

"You do not, nor does your presence interfere with my plans," answered Phileas Fogg, coldly.

Misses Aouda, who was in awe of such a determined gentleman, accepted his sincere invite to accompany him on his incredible journey.

Hong Kong could be Fix's last chance to arrest Mister Fogg on his suspicious journey around the world. They would not be on British territory after that, so he would only be able to detain Mister Fogg upon his return to England. But did he plan on returning to London? Fix did not want to run that risk. As the arrest warrant had not arrived, he decided to delay the gentleman's journey by distracting Passepartout, so the inspector invited him for a stroll around the city. The Frenchman wandered through the streets, enchanted by the novelties and array of lights and colours.

Suddenly Passepartout realised he was alone and lost in a labyrinth of alleyways. The further he walked, the more confused he got. Would he be able to return to the ship in time for its departure?

The next day, November 7, Mister Fogg arrived at the quay to board the *Carnatic*, but he learnt something terrible: the repairs on the ship had been completed sooner than expected and it had already sailed to Japan. To make matters worse, Passepartout was not there. What happened to his servant: was he lost in the city or did he board the ship? Had his journey around the world in eighty days been jeopardised?

9 Risky maneuvers in the east

DESPITE NOT HAVING BOARDED THE CARNATIC, the ship that would have taken them to Yokohama, and with no sign of Passepartout's whereabouts, Mister Fogg remained calm. He walked along the docks searching for another means of transport. He had to arrive in Yo-kohama in time to board the *General Grant*, a steamer that was going to cross the Pacific Ocean to the United States.

Inspector Fix had been following Mister Fogg, hoping he would be delayed. But the winds were favourable for the determined gentleman. As he walked along the docks, he met the master of a sailboat and asked:

"Do you know how I can get to Yokohama, Japan, by the 14th? I must take a boat to San Francisco."

"I'm sorry! That is too dangerous for my precious *Tankadère*," replied the old sailor, then added, "but I can take you to Shanghai on the coast of *China*. Not only is it a safer route, but that is where the American ship sets sail from. Later the ship will put in at Yokohama."

"Perfect. It's a deal."

At 3.10 pm on November 7 the brave steamer set sail to Hong Kong as if it were in a boat race. Mister Fogg, Aouda and the relentless Fix were on the main deck. The inspector did not want to lose sight of his suspect, so he accepted the invitation to sail along the coast, and Phileas Fogg did not suspect a thing. Mister Fogg still had hopes of meeting Passepartout on the next stop of their journey.

Soon the wind began to blow hard and the sea became rough. The storm gained strength by nightfall. The *Tankadère* bravely faced the tall threatening waves. The hands of the clock also seemed to become rough, as if they were moving faster. Four days had passed in the rough sea. On November 11 they approached the port of Shanghai, where they saw a ship sailing on the horizon, as if signalling that Phileas Fogg's plans were leaving: the *General Grant* had just left for America!

"Flag at half-mast! Fire!" ordered Mister Fogg without a second thought.

The sound of the small cannon could be heard miles away. Mister Fogg knew that those were nautical signals of distress for another ship to come help. They were acting as if it was an emergency. And in a way it was, especially for Phileas Fogg, a gentleman in an incredible race around the world.

The plan had worked: a few minutes later, after they were rescued from the sailboat, the trio was comfortably settled in the American steamer headed to Yokohama and then San Francisco. Fix was constantly at the heels of Phileas Fogg, who continued to reign over time, as if the hours and minutes were his subjects.

When they reached the Japanese port of Yokohama after an uneventful journey, Mister Fogg and Aouda disembarked to try to find Passepartout. Was he still in Hong Kong or did he manage to get on the *Carnatic*? They went to see the authorities and were given some good news: the Frenchman's name was on the list of passengers! Yet, he was not on board, so Phileas Fogg went to search for his servant. He went to the French consulate and wandered the streets of the city in vain: there was no sign of Passepartout.

With no alternatives left, they returned to the port. However, just before boarding with Misses Aouda, they came upon a performance in front of the *General Grant*, where they watched a great acrobatic show: a pyramid formed of men with large noses and wings that looked like playing cards.

The crowd was applauding enthusiastically as the drums rolled. Suddenly, the pyramid fell apart. No wonder: one of the men leapt out, screaming…

"Master! My master!"

Mister Fogg and Misses Aouda immediately recognised Passepartout falling amid all the other men with long noses, as if a castle of cards came tumbling down. Later they learnt what had happened: the servant arrived in Japan on the *Carnatic* and looked for employment to earn some money to travel on the *General Grant* and reunite with them. Since he told people that he was a great acrobat, he got the job. Yet, during the best part of the show he tumbled down and practically fell in his master's lap!
   On November 14 the three of them boarded the majestic white American steamer. Unbeknownst to them, another passenger climbed on board as well: the unstoppable Inspector Fix!

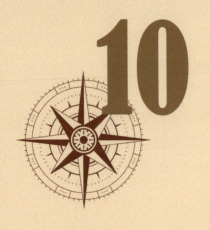

10 A long adventure in the railways across America

DESPITE THE VASTNESS OF THE LARGEST OCEAN IN THE WORLD, the Pacific Ocean justified its name: it took the *General Grant* almost three long weeks to cross it, and it went quite smoothly. On December 3, when half of the journey around the world had been completed, Phileas Fogg arrived in San Francisco on the west coast of America. According to his calculations, he had not lost a single day.

At seven o'clock in the morning, when they set foot in California, the French servant committed yet another blunder. Passepartout was overjoyed to arrive in a new continent, so he showed it by performing a vault onto American ground. To his dismay, he landed on some rotten wooden boards and fell right through them. His acrobatic performance turned into a circus clown performance!

After many days at sea, from now on their long journey ahead would continue on land. They must cross the United States and reach New York on a very long railroad ride. The train they had to catch for the next part of their journey would only leave at night, so they had time to visit the city of San Francisco. They were baffled by the wide streets, the low and perfectly aligned houses, the curious horse-drawn trams, giant warehouses that looked like palaces, and sidewalks crowded with people from all over the world.

Mister Fogg headed over to the consulate to have his passport stamped and found Inspector Fix there. Any other person would have found the inspector's presence a bit strange, but Phileas Fogg did not even blink. The inspector, on the other hand, feigned surprise at seeing them there and invited himself to accompany them once again. Since they were not on British territory, it would be more difficult to arrest the man he believed to be a great robber.

The only thing he could do was to make sure Mister Fogg returned to England. Meanwhile, Passepartout considered punching the inspector in the face because he was the reason he got lost in Hong Kong. Fix had taken him to the middle of a labyrinth, then left him. But Passepartout did not want to cause problems for his master, so he decided to keep it to himself.

They stepped onto the Oakland train platform at 5.45 pm; it was the starting point of a long adventure across the country. Exactly fifteen minutes later, the train's sharp whistle blew, and it left the station and headed towards the east coast. "From ocean to ocean" is what the six-thousand-kilometre railroad was called, and it connected the entire span of the United States of America. Not long ago, it took at least six months to travel from coast to coast, but now, with the railway divided in three routes, it was done in seven days. That was good timing for the Englishman: he would have enough time to reach New York to take the ship to Liverpool on December 11.

The train travelled along the railroad towards Ogden, Utah, the first stretch of the journey. It wound around the mountainsides and road along precipices, never slowing down. The train's whistle and loud noise mingled with the sounds of waterfalls and torrential rivers.

Suddenly, another loud noise coming from outside drew the passengers' attention. Actually, it was not one but rather many sounds. Around ten thousand buffaloes marched alongside the train, which had to come to a stop. They had come to the vast prairies of the State of Nevada, where buffaloes formed actual moving currents that could block railroads. On that day, a herd of buffaloes blocked Mister Fogg's passage.

Passepartout watched impatiently from his window. As he was more engaged in his master's adventure, the angry Frenchman scolded the animals, the United States and the conductor.

"What kind of country is this, where animals stop the trains? Why doesn't the conductor run the train into the herd? What a waste of time!" he cried.

Phileas Fogg sat in his seat, calmly waiting for the parade of buffaloes to pass, although it seemed endless and might affect his plans. He was not annoyed. But would he be able to make up for the lost time during the rest of the journey to New York? Boats can navigate more effectively with favourable winds, but not trains. Was there a way to gain time?

11 Snow might freeze Phileas Fogg's plans

After waiting for three long hours, the train set off again in the middle of the night. The next day, December 6, they got off at Ogden and decided to go for a walk. The train would only depart to Omaha, in the heart of the country and the next stretch of their long journey across the United States, in the afternoon. Ogden was built the same way as other American cities: its long straight lines looked like a checker-board. Fix pretended to be the perfect adventure companion and was always at Fogg's side.

Travelling across the State of Utah was uneventful. Not even the snow delayed the train. All of a sudden it stopped, but this time it was not because of animals…

"We cannot pass! The bridge at Medicine Bow is shaky and will not support the weight of the train," announced the signalman. They would have to go to the next station on foot, which meant walking through the snow for six hours! This news caused many passengers to protest, and soon there was shouting along the railroad until…

"I have a solution!" called out the engineer. "If the train pulls off at full speed from a distance, we have a chance of crossing the bridge. I believe the speed will compensate for the weight because it will reduce the pressure on the damaged structure."

The passengers disregarded the danger involved in that crazy suggestion and seemed very interested in the engineer's proposal: they desperately wanted to leave that freezing place and reach their destination. They all returned to their places in the cars, the train backed up about two kilometres, then pushed forward like an enraged bull. It soon reached the speed of one hundred and fifty km per hour, and crossed the river like a flash of lightning. It was only able to come to a complete stop after it had gone eight kilometres on the other side. As soon as the last car passed over the river, however, the bridge fell and crashed into the raging waters of the Medicine Bow River.

That was not their last scare; on the contrary, there were many surprises on the train ride to Nebraska. The worst scare was a terrifying attack by thieves who tried to rob the cargo and the passengers' belongings on the train. They arrived in bands mounted on horses, surrounded the train on both sides and tried to climb inside the moving cars. Amidst gunshots and stones raining down upon it, the valiant train plunged forward and maintained its course. Later, however, the conductor had no choice but to stop in Fort Kearney station, as there were many injured passengers and damaged cars.

Fortunately, Phileas Fogg and his travel companions were not hurt. The gentleman's plans, however, suffered a major setback: after so many obstacles, there was only one train to take them to Omaha the following day!

There was going to be a delay of twenty hours, and Phileas Fogg would not arrive in New York in time to board the ship back to England. He barely knew how to get to Omaha! He stood motionless. Misses Aouda was inconsolable. Passepartout also feared for his master. The snow would not melt; the winds blew fierce and strong. Yet, these very winds could save the plans of the composed Englishman. Fix, who wished to arrive quickly in London to arrest his suspect, had a surprising and unique solution. A citizen of Fort Kearney named Mudge had invented a strange way of transport for when the trains could not travel along frozen railroads: a sledge with sails!

Mister Fogg wasted no time and made arrangements to use the curious vehicle, and they quickly left the small hut next to Fort Kearney. The prairies seemed like a vast carpet of ice upon which the sledge easily skimmed over, captained by its agile pilot Mudge. Not even the starving wolves, running and howling after the sledge, could gain distance on them. They finally reached Omaha. They had just enough time to jump on a moving train car, which would take them to Chicago. The next day was December 10 and they had just passed through the State of Iowa at incredible speed. It was 4 o'clock in the afternoon when they arrived at the huge station in Chicago, the main city of the State of Illinois. There were many trains leaving Chicago, so Mister Fogg easily found a connection to New York.

The mighty train travelled across the States of Indiana, Ohio, Pennsylvania and New Jersey in a flash, as if it knew its illustrious passenger was in a hurry. By the time the Hudson River came into view along the famous American city, it was late at night on December 11. At 11.15 pm they arrived at the station in New York, in front of the harbour where the ships left to Europe. But…

The steamer *China* had left for Liverpool forty-five minutes ago!

12 The exciting voyage across the Atlantic ocean

The *China* seemed to have taken Phileas Fogg's last hopes with it. In fact, none of the other steamers were headed for Europe anytime soon. Time seemed to be working against the gentleman. But he did not appear to be worried; he merely decided they should get a good nights' sleep in a hotel.

The next morning at 7 o'clock, December 12, Mister Fogg left the hotel alone and headed towards the harbour. On December 21 at 8.45 pm he had to be on the other side of the Atlantic Ocean, at the Reform Club in London. Therefore, he had nine days, thirteen hours and forty-five minutes to get there. If he had boarded the *China*, he would have plenty of time to make his appointment. The clock did not stop ticking, and it was only drowned by the sound of a horn coming from a cargo ship that was almost ready to set out to sea. Its name: *Henrietta*. Destination: Bordeaux, France. Its captain, Speedy, was getting the boat ready to weigh anchor.

After bargaining for a long time, Fogg arranged with Captain Speedy to take them to… France! Oops, France? Weren't they going to England? The trio that accompanied the determined member of the Reform Club had been asking themselves that question for hours, but they would come to understand his plans in time.

It was 9 o'clock, not long after, when Mister Fogg, Misses Aouda, Passepartout and Inspector Fix were on the modest *Henrietta*.

The voyage and the unpredictable ocean foreshadowed twists. The first one was put forth the next morning: guess who presented himself as the newly named captain…

None other than Phileas Fogg! The new destination: Liverpool! Captain Speedy was secured in his cabin under lock and key, from which shouts and cursing could be heard. The crew was tired of being mistreated by the old captain, so they went along with the determined English gentleman.

The first days of the voyage across the Atlantic Ocean were calm. Things seemed to be working in favour of the cold and calculating Englishman. Fix had no idea what was going on, and he could only wait to see what would happen. Misses Aouda mostly kept to herself, but she was increasingly delighted with Mister Fogg's adventures. And Passepartout, well, he befriended the sailors and helped them manage the boat.

On December 13, when they passed along the coast of Newfoundland, the ocean's winds and currents changed, signalling revolt. An endless storm retarded *Henrietta*'s progress, and it was necessary to furl the sails and

move forwards only with the force of the coal-fuelled motors. However, a lot of coal was needed to face the tall waves and plunge ahead, so it didn't take long for them to be out of the precious coal.

The captain had no choice but to burn everything on board and use it instead of coal: armoires, beds, barrels, curtains, frames, chairs, and what was left of the upper deck. But this was only done with the approval of *Henrietta*'s owner, who was finally set free from his imprisonment. In exchange, Mister Fogg paid Captain Speedy a fortune for burning his boat. This way he could keep his hopes up to complete his journey around the world within the time limit.

As the weather continued to be an impediment, time seemed to hinder them as well. According to his calculations, Phileas Fogg realized they would not drop anchor at Liverpool on the date he had planned. After all, it was 10 pm on December 20, and they had barely reached the coast of the island of Ireland, which was on the route to England. They still had a long way to go, and besides, he was not sure the boat would make it since it looked like a floating bonfire.

It was dark when suddenly they saw promising lights on the horizon. Captain Speedy announced they were near the port of Queenstown on the Irish coast. When Phileas Fogg learnt that there was an express train connecting this city to the capital on the other side of the island, he calculated that it would gain precious time if he took this short cut on land.

Once they arrived in the harbour, he and his companions went on shore at once, and in a few minutes they were travelling on the train from Queenstown to Dublin. Then, from Ireland's capital, they were able to reach one of the fast steamers headed to Liverpool.

Phileas Fogg finally set foot on English soil at 11.40 am on December 21. They were in Liverpool, which was a few hours away from London. But at that moment, Inspector Fix came up to Mister Fogg, placed his hand on his shoulder as per British tradition, and, showing his much awaited warrant, asked, "Are you really Phileas Fogg?"

"Yes, sir!"

"In the name of the Queen, you are under arrest!"

13 Is it the end of the line for Phileas Fogg?

PHILEAS FOGG WAS UNDER ARREST. The gentleman was detained in the Customs Office in Liverpool, where he was to spend the rest of the day. Passepartout could not contain his anger and attacked the treacherous inspector. He wanted to pull out his hair, moustache, beard… But instead he was pulled away by two policemen. Misses Aouda was greatly disturbed, and she protested in vain. As for Inspector Fix, he had accomplished his mission, whether Mister Fogg was guilty or not. The courts would decide.

Mister Fogg sat motionless on a wooden bench in his cell, studying his watch on the table. He, that had controlled time until now, felt as if the second hands were escaping him, taking with them his chances of winning the wager. The cathedral bell chimed loudly, as if announcing his failure.

At 2.33 pm the cell door flung open with a loud thud, and Misses Aouda, Passepartout and Fix bustled in.

"Sir, I beg your pardon… an amazing coincidence… the real bank robber… England… was found and arrested. You are… free!" announced Inspector Fix, out of breath. For the first time Mister Fogg showed his feelings and punched the inspector in the face.

"Great punch!" cried Passepartout, feeling he was getting revenge.

Mister Fogg did not spare one second before collecting his watch and practically throwing himself

53

inside a cab, which took him, the young lady and the loyal servant to the station. The express train had already left for London, so he had to order a special train, and at 3 o'clock in the afternoon they left for the capital.

However, luck seemed to go off the rails: the train had to slow down and even come to a complete stop several times along the way. They arrived at the central station when all the clocks in London where showing 8.50 pm, five minutes past the time the gentleman had to be at the Reform Club. Phileas Fogg had lost the wager!

The next day, the house at No. 7 Saville Row appeared to be empty. No sounds were heard, no lights were on. There was no sign of inhabitants: not Phileas Fogg nor his noble guest and not even Passepartout. They spent the entire day in recluse, motionless like the furniture, overwhelmed at their misfortune.

Defeated! That was what Phileas Fogg felt. After travelling the long journey around the world, overcoming uncountable obstacles, facing many dangers, and even doing good deeds along the way, after all of that… He had lost the battle against time. He had used a good portion of his money on the journey, and after paying the wager, he would not have much left. Not only defeated, but ruined as well! There was no reason for him to present himself, late, to his friends at the Reform Club. He had lost. He only had to pay the wager at the bank, nothing else. It was over.

There was only one bright note on that sad and dark Sunday, when Mister Fogg went to the room he had reserved for Misses Aouda to speak with her in private.

"Pardon me, Misses Aouda, for bringing you to England," he said after several minutes of silence. "Madam, allow me to be at your service, with the little I have left, and offer you a dignified life."

"Mister Fogg," replied Misses Aouda, looking into his eyes and firmly holding one of the hands of the man who saved her life, "you have not only shown bravery, but generosity too, for you have a big heart which has conquered me. I want to be your wife; will you marry me?"

"Yes, I love you!" replied Phileas Fogg. "I love you more than anything in the world!"

Passepartout was summoned, and upon entering the room his master ordered him to find Reverend Samuel Wilson of the Mary-le- Bone parish at once. He wanted a simple ceremony to be held on Monday.

"Tomorrow?" he asked, turning to Misses Aouda.

"Yes, tomorrow, Monday!" confirmed the young lady. Passepartout ran through the dark streets of London in a hurry to reach the parish.

Dishevelled, he told Reverend Samuel Wilson what he was requested to do.

"I need you to perform a wedding tomorrow." The Reverend looked at Passepartout in surprise and said, "A wedding cannot be performed tomorrow, young man!"

"Why not? Tomorrow is Monday!"

"No, sir, tomorrow is Sunday!"

The young Frenchman almost fell in shock. It was hard to believe, but Mister Fogg had made a mistake of one day, and they arrived twenty-four hours ahead of time!

Passepartout returned to the house like a train running over everything along its path. When he arrived at No. 7 Saville Row, almost one whole day had passed since they had stepped onto the station in London. It was 8.35 pm now: only ten minutes before the clock struck 8.45, when his master had vowed to be at the Reform Club!

Phileas Fogg only had time to grab his hat and Misses Aouda's arm. On the way, they saw a coachman fixing his broken horse-drawn cab.

14 The anticipation of Mister Fogg's arrival at the Reform Club and in Egland

IT IS IMPORTANT TO NOTE WHAT HAD OCCURRED IN BRITAIN, especially after the robber of the Bank of England had been arrested in Edinburgh on December 17. Until that time, Phileas Fogg was the main suspect, and his journey around the world was considered a clever ploy for the gentleman to run away with the money. Once the real robber was caught, everyone believed in Phileas Fogg; most people even cheered for him.

This story was in every newspaper. Ladies and gentlemen ran to the streets of England hoping to hear more news of the eccentric gentleman. His friends at the Reform Club spent the last few days in a state of unease. The day the robber was arrested was the seventy- sixth day after Phileas Fogg's departure on his journey around the world. Everyone repeatedly asked if the noble Englishman would arrive at the saloon in the club on Saturday, December 21, at 8.45 pm.

The anticipation increased each day; however, there was no news of Mister Fogg. Was he in Asia? Was he in America? No one had a clue. Not even the police knew the whereabouts of Inspector Fix, who was supposed to be following the apparent suspect.

On December 21, when Phileas Fogg was scheduled to arrive at the Reform Club, London was at a standstill. A large crowd outside the noble building in Pall Mall

and neighbouring streets waited for Phileas Fogg to arrive. His five friends were gathered in the saloon in the club. The bankers John Sullivan and Samuel Fallentin, the engineer Andrew Stuart, the director of the Bank of England Gauthier Ralph, and the brewer Thomas Flanagan were the most anxious of all in the country. The clock showed 8.25.

"Gentlemen, in twenty minutes the time agreed upon with Mister Fogg will have expired," announced Andrew Stuart, as he stood up.

"We have no news from him. Phileas Fogg's name was not among those on the list of passengers on board the *China*," added John Sullivan.

"This was a crazy idea from the start. There was no way he could have predicted inevitable delays along the way," continued Thomas Flanagan.

"I'm sure tomorrow we will receive a check for the wager. He lost!" said Gauthier Ralph.

As the men spoke, the hands on the clock showed 8.40. There were only five minutes left. They looked at each other impatiently. They thought of Phileas Fogg's reserved behaviour. His journey, as well as his life, were surrounded by mystery. They were getting more nervous by the minute.

"It's 8.43!" said Thomas Flanagan a few minutes later.

No one moved in the Reform Club. But the crowd outside was restless, and shrill screams could be heard.

"It's 8.44!" said John Sullivan, breathing heavily.

The second hand on the clock in the great saloon began its final round.

Only fifty seconds left. Forty. Thirty seconds.

No one said a word. No one breathed. Everyone stared at the closed door. Twenty. Ten seconds to go…

15 The only error made by the methodical Phileas Fogg

WITH ONLY FIVE SECONDS LEFT, the door of the great saloon opened and… "Here I am, gentlemen!" Phileas Fogg entered, followed by the excited crowd that had been waiting outside, screaming and applauding.

Seeing the looks of surprise on his friends' faces, he added, "Yes, Phileas Fogg himself!"

Mister Fogg had won his incredible wager. He was able to complete his journey around the world in eighty days!

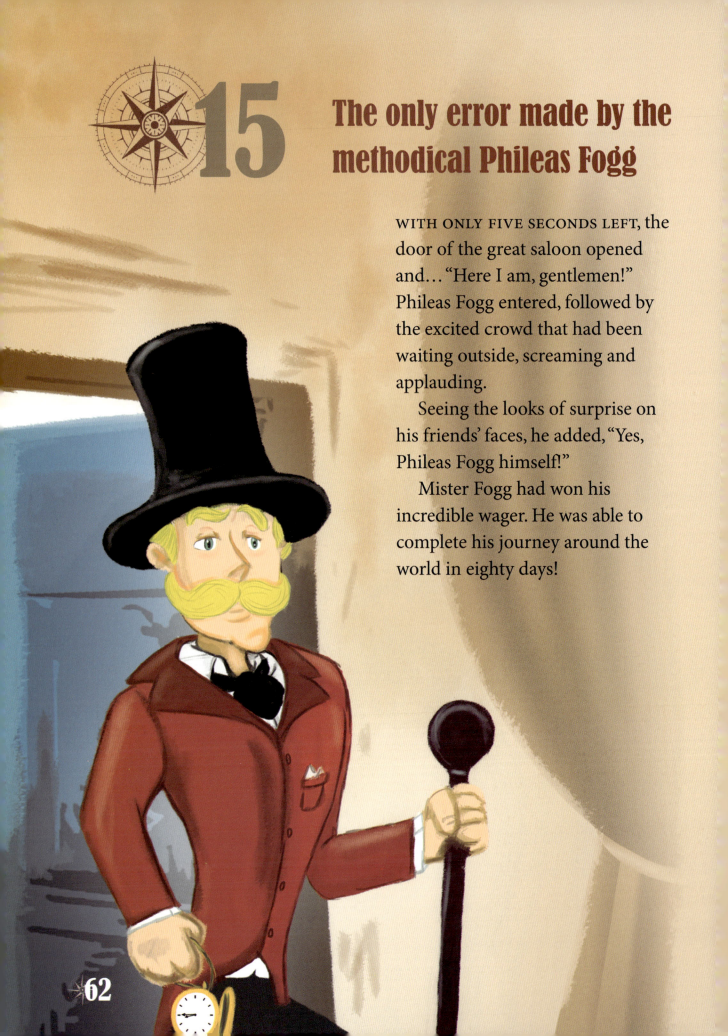

Dear reader, you must also have been surprised by the incredible Phileas Fogg. After all, what happened? What error did he make in his calculations? It is very simple. In fact, it is so simple that even the methodical Englishman missed it. Mister Fogg was not aware that he would gain one day on his journey solely because he went around the world. In fact, by travelling eastward, towards the sun, the days grew shorter by four minutes each time he crossed a degree in that direction. Multiply the three hundred and sixty degrees of the circumference of the Earth by four minutes, and you will get twenty-four hours, which is one day!

To put it another way, Phileas Fogg, as he travelled eastward, saw the sun pass the meridian eighty times, while his friends at the Reform Club saw it seventy-nine times. That is why that day was Saturday instead of Sunday, as the gentleman initially thought.

Anyhow, what did Phileas Fogg gain from his journey around the world? What did he accomplish along this journey?

Some would say nothing was gained, but is that true? We must not forget that he had the opportunity to see a world that is rich in cultural diversity, and he met a charming woman who made him the happiest man in the world!

JULES VERNE, the author of this book, was born in Nantes, France, in 1828. He was the oldest of five brothers, and his father wanted him to take over the family business. Therefore, he studied law in Nantes, then continued his studies in Paris. But Jules loved literature and art. Starting at the age of ten, he always carried a pencil and paper with him to draw and write. Through his acquaintance with Alexandre Dumas, he worked in the theatre and became known to the public. Soon his work was noticed by Jules Hetzel, an editor who saw Verne's talent for literature. His first romance novel, *Five Weeks in a Balloon*, launched the author's career to soaring heights. Later he published *Around the World in 80 Days*, *Twenty Thousand Leagues Under the Sea*, *Journey to the Centre of the Earth*, *From the Earth to the Moon* and *The Mysterious Island*. He was one of the great pioneers of science fiction during an era of great inventions (19th century) such as electricity, the telephone, steamboat and railways.

BETO JUNQUEYRA adapted this book. He grew up reading books by Monteiro Lobato and Jules Verne, living in farms in Minas Gerais and villas in northern Portugal. At the age of nine he wrote short stories, and after travelling to many places around the world and gaining many ideas, he wrote his first children's book *Volta ao mundo falando português*, inspired by Jules Verne's book. He also wrote *Deu a louca no mundo*, *Pintou sujeira!*, *Ecopiratas em Fernando de Noronha* and *Quem tem boca vai ao Timor*, among other works.

DANILO TANAKA illustrated this work. He was born in the South Zone of São Paulo, and he has loved drawing from an early age. He took his first drawing classes when he was twelve, and at thirteen he won his first prize, a "Special Merit Award". He uses many different styles of painting and drawing. He has a BA degree in Advertising and an MBA in Marketing, and he won the ABF + RDI Design Award for Packaging in 2016 and 2017.